Thank you to everyone who helped make this book happen, especially:

My parents, Paul and Belinda Schlack
Dr. Lindsey Pollock at Rolling Hills Veterinary Clinic
Steve Shannon
Brian Morrison

I must acknowledge the dedicated hard work of the stars of the book, **Peter Cat and Berry Dog.**

And last but never least, thank you to my husband, **Ted Shannon**, for all the things you do.

Please support your local animal shelter.

When you decide that it is time to bring a new pet into your home, consider adopting from your local animal shelter. It is true that you cannot save them all, and that the world will not change just because you adopt a pet. But for the pet you adopt, their world will surely change.

Almost Home Project

www.almosthomeproject.petfinder.com

Black and White CAT
White and Black DOG

Written and Illustrated by
Marlaena Shannon
Designed by Joli Winsett

Muse Direct Publishing

When they first met, black and white cat thought that white

and black dog was very big, and very loud,

and much too nosey.

White and black dog thought that black and white cat was much too full of sharp and pointy parts for such a small thing.

They kept away from each other for a very long time.

Until:

One dinner time, black and white cat climbed up his cat tree to find food, but there was nothing in his dish!

How alarming!

Then, he heard a can opener opening a can in the kitchen. All cats know that cans have food
inside. So, he jumped down and trotted into the kitchen to see.

Black and white cat found white and black dog's dish.

It was full of food!   It smelled pretty good, too.

White and black dog saw black and white cat eating her food.

What do you suppose happened next?

White and black dog shared her food with black and white cat.

What a nice thing to do.   Are you surprised?

After dinner, black and white cat always gave himself a bath.   White and black dog noticed that
black and white cat smelled like dog food.   She decided to help him with his bath.

So, she licked him.   He didn't seem to mind.

Since then, they have been friends.

They look out the same window together.

They share toys,

treats,

bath time,

hiding places,

art,

music,

and bugs.

When white and black dog goes out for walks, black and white cat waits
in the window watching until he returns.

When black and white cat gets stuck in the closet, which is quite often, white and black dog will not come away from the door until he is let out.

White and black dog tries not to be as loud and nosey as she used to.

And black and white cat tries to be less sharp and pointy than he used to.

Which do you think happened first:

Did a dog and a cat become best friends because
they were always a little bit alike?

Or, did they each become a little bit like the other
when they decided to be friends?

Perhaps it does not
matter either way.
One thing is certain:

How lucky they are to
be forever friends.

The End.